# The Puzzling Puzzles

Bothersome Games Which Will Bother Some People

HarperEntertainment

*An Imprint of* HarperCollins*Publishers*

## A Note About the Answers

There are many things I do not know. I do not know why the Baudelaire children have been visited with such terrible misfortune at such a young age. I do not know why Count Olaf is such a cruel, vile, greedy villain. I do not know what is contained within nougat, a beige, fluffy ingredient in some candy bars.

But I do know the answers to most of the activities, games, and vitally important secret codes contained within this field training guide, and I have hidden them in the back of this book in case of emergency.

I would wish you good luck, but it would be unwise to say such a thing, in light of everything I know. I will, however, extend my Very Fond Desires for the safe and successful completion of your training. More people are watching your progress than you know I know you know, and not all of them are pleasant.

You might as well begin now.


L.S.

# PERPLEXING PICTURE

### How many fire extinguishers can you find in this picture?

# MYSTIFYING MAZE

Help the Baudelaire children
find a happy home.

Start

# ENIGMATIC ENIGMA

If you complete this series of clues by answering these trivia questions, you will be rewarded with an important secret message.

1. In which country near Australia are you likely to find a bird called a notornis?  N _ _  _ _ _ _ _ _ D

2. What is the capital of the answer to #1?

_ _ L L _ _ _ _ O _

3. The answer to #2 is also the name of a popular beef dish. What culinary element, also found in pizza, does this dish feature? _ _ _ S T

4. The answer to #3 is also a common name for the layer of rock that covers the earth. What is a fancier name?

_ I _ _ O S P H _ _ _

5. How many letters are in the word that is the answer to #4?

# LABORIOUS LANGUAGE GAME
## If you do not know how to complete this activity, you would be better off buying some other book.

ACROSS

3. Something to clean or jump out of

4. Furniture under which things are often hidden

9. Iguana, snake, etc.

10. Lemon-y

12. Parent replacement

14. The opposite of disguise

15. In the Sebald Code, the number of spoken words between every coded word

18. This sort of puzzle

19. A country where you may find Lima beans

20. Something used to hold a snake or a baby


DOWN

1. An important secret acronym

2. To abduct

5. Olaf's emblem, of which you probably have two

6. The study of how words are used in a sentence

7. What you do before burying something in the backyard

8. Rhymes with low

11. Sound signaling beginning and ending of a Sebald Code transmission

13. Fire starter

16. A group of actors

17. Things read by the intelligent

# CONVOLUTED CRAFT
## Make a blindfold to shield your eyes in the event you are forced to attend a theater showing
### LEMONY SNICKET'S A SERIES OF UNFORTUNATE EVENTS.

*Step 1.* Ask your parent or guardian if you have permission to use scissors.

*Step 2.* If they say yes, cut out the black shape on the opposite page. BE SURE TO SOLVE THE ACTIVITIES ON THE FLIP SIDE OF THE OPPOSITE PAGE FIRST OR THE BLIND-FOLD WILL NOT WORK.

*Step 3.* Place the cut-out shape on an enormous bolt of black blind-fold cloth.

*Step 4.* Measure all the way around your head using a twelve-inch wooden ruler (English system) or metre stick (metric system, English spelling).

*Step 5.* Add four inches or 10.16 centimetres to the length measured in Step 4.

*Step 6.* Subtract 7.63 inches or 19.38 centimetres from the length arrived at in Step 5.

*Step 7.* Measure the distance arrived at in Step 6 from one end of the cut-out shape on your enormous bolt of black blindfold cloth.

*Step 8.* Mark with a pencil.

*Step 9.* Cut out the resulting rectangular shape. If you completed Steps 2–8 correctly, the resulting piece of blindfold cloth should be longer than the cut-out shape.

*Step 10.* Wrap the piece of cloth around your head, covering your eyes.

*Step 11.* Using one thumb and one forefinger on the same hand, pinch the ends of the cloth together at the back of your head.

*Step 12.* Hold.

*Step 13.* If you can read Steps 11–15, return to Step 10.

*Step 14.* Now what do you see?

*Step 15.* Good.

# LABORIOUS LANGUAGE GAME

Fill in the correct letters to complete these sentences.

1. If the authorities ever capture Count Olaf, he should be put in __ a __l.

2. Violet Baudelaire sometimes __ __ __ ents things when she is in a difficult situation.

3. Klaus Baudelaire can frequently be found __ __ ading __ __ oks, sometimes with his sister Violet.

# TERMINAL TRIVIA

How many Baudelaire siblings are there?

# PERPLEXING PICTURE

## What's wrong with this picture?

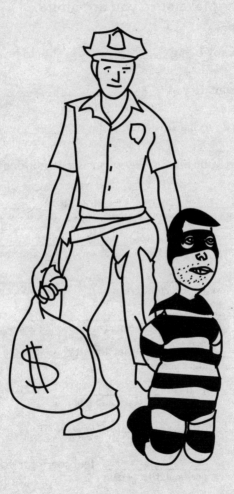

# LABORIOUS LANGUAGE GAME

Fill in each of the blanks with the type of word
or phrase indicated, and then read
what you have created aloud.
Make sure you are alone.

Unless you enjoy being _____, you should probably
<u>adjective</u>

_____ this page. If you _____ a _____
<u>verb</u>        <u>verb, present perfect</u>    <u>noun</u>

before, you know that it is among the _____
<u>adverb, irregular superlative</u>

ways to spend your time, since it consists of nothing but

_____ , _____ , _____, and more _____ .
<u>noun, plural</u>  <u>noun, plural</u>  <u>noun, plural</u>        <u>noun, plural</u>

_____ , some people _____
<u>adverb, conjunctive</u>          <u>verb, auxiliary progressive</u>

entertained by _____ words _____
<u>verb, perfect progressive</u>      <u>preposition, phrasal</u>

_____ . If _____ are one of
<u>noun, plural</u>  <u>pronoun, subjective personal, second person</u>

them, you _____ this activity _____
<u>verb, future perfect</u>          <u>preposition, simple</u>

_____ in all of ____ _____ . You are clearly
<u>verb, progressive</u>        <u>article</u> <u>noun, plural</u>

the _____ of _____ activities, and
<u>noun, proper</u>      <u>adjective</u>

_____ feel sorry for you.
<u>pronoun, subjective personal, first person</u>

# ENIGMATIC ENIGMA
Use the Helquist Code (1=a, 2=b, 3=c, etc.)
to decipher an extremely sensitive secret message.

22 15 12 21 14 20 5 5 18 19   14 5 5 4 5 4

16 12 5 1 19 5   3 15 14 20 9 14 21 5

# PERPLEXING PICTURE
These close-up images are all
people you should know. Who are they?

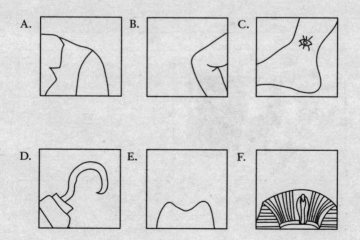

A.    B.    C.

D.    E.    F.

# PERPLEXING PICTURE
## Which of these people are in disguise?

# MUDDLING MATH TASK

Mr. Poe gives Klaus Baudelaire $11.50 to buy whatever he wants from a bookstore that sells only eight books. Klaus chooses WHY BAD THINGS HAPPEN TO GOOD CHILDREN and THE PARTIALLY COMPLETE ENGLISH DICTIONARY. What else can he buy?

Now Selling

*Why Bad Things Happen to Good Children* — $3.95

*The Littlest Elf Goes to Hollywood* — $4.50

*Cucumber Soup for the Orphan Soul* — $3.75

*Giggles Make You Happy! The Littlest Elf's Two Steps to a Jolly Life* — $3.85

*Putting the Fortune in Misfortune: An Introduction to Inheritance Management* — $5.50

*VFD Field Training Guide* — $1,667.79

*The Littlest Elf's Songs to Skip To* — $3.60

*The Partially Complete English Dictionary (A–E)* — $4.20

# CONVOLUTED CRAFT

Follow these instructions to make Pasta
Puttanesca, which the Baudelaire children
cooked for Count Olaf and his acting troupe, who
were ungrateful.

*Step 1.* Ask your parent or guardian for permission to use their credit card.

*Step 2.* Drive yourself to the grocery store. Park with caution.

*Step 3.* In the frozen food aisle, locate Pasta Puttanesca.

*Step 4.* If there is no Pasta Puttanesca, return home.

*Step 5.* Ask your parent or guardian if you have the following ingredients:

> 2 large water balloons, full
>
> $^3/_8$ cup extremely virgin olive oil
>
> 3 barely medium-sized cloves of garlic
>
> $2^1/_2$ pinches of dried red chili pepper flakes
>
> 1 woodsman's handful of black olives
>
> 5 anchovy fillets
>
> $^1/_2$ thimble of dried oregano
>
> 1 bunch of fresh parsley
>
> $1^1/_2$ pounds of unrotten tomatoes
>
> 2 youngster palmfuls of capers, squeezed tightly to drain

*Step 6.* If your parent or guardian reveals that you do not have any of these ingredients, return to the grocery store.

*Step 7.* Purchase any ingredients that are outstanding, a word which here means "missing" rather than "of exceptional quality." Return home.

*Step 8.* Ask your parent or guardian if you may use a sharp knife. If the answer is no, ask if you may use a dull one.

*Step 9.* Prepare the following ingredients by following the following instructions:

    a. Peel and slice the garlic cloves.

    b. Pit and dice the olives.

    c. Cut the anchovy fillets into little pieces.

    d. Finely tear up the parsley and measure out 4 tablespoons.

    e. Peel, seed, and chop the tomatoes.

*Step 10.* Ask your parent or guardian if you have permission to use the stove.

*Step 11.* If you have permission, follow the preparation of ingredients with the following of the following instructions:

    a. Break the water balloons into a pot of water and boil. Be sure to remove the balloons.

    b. Heat the extremely virgin olive oil in a big skillet.

    c. Add the garlic and red chili pepper flakes.

    d. Stir for exactly 40 seconds.

    e. Add the olives, anchovies, and oregano, and cook for exactly 35 seconds.

    f. Stir in the tomatoes.

    g. Simmer on low heat, uncovered, for exactly 5 minutes and 15 seconds.

    h. Throw in the parsley and the capers.

    i. Add as much black pepper as you want.

*Step 12.* Oh! The pasta! Run and ask your parent or guardian if you have pasta.

*Step 13.* If you don't, drive yourself to the grocery store and get some. Be sure to turn off the stove or your home may burn down. Return home.

*Step 14.* Place one pound of pasta in the pot of boiling water.

*Step 15.* Cook until al dente, an Italian phrase which here means "like soft licorice."

*Step 16.* Toss pasta with sauce.

*Step 17.* Serve hot, from the left, wearing an apron and using a fork or, if necessary, chopsticks.

# LABORIOUS LANGUAGE GAME

How many different words can be made out of the letters in the phrase "LEMONY SNICKET'S A SERIES OF UNFORTUNATE EVENTS gives me a stomachache"?

_____     _____     _____

_____     _____     _____

_____     _____     _____

_____     _____     _____

_____     _____     _____

_____     _____     _____

_____     _____     _____

_____     _____     _____

_____     _____     _____

_____     _____     _____

_____     _____     _____

_____     _____     _____

_____     _____     _____

_____     _____     _____

# PERPLEXING PICTURE

Find the nine spyglasses in this picture.

# PERPLEXING PICTURE

Connect the dots to see what is widely believed
to be the home of an esteemed citizen
before it was consumed by a terrible fire.

# MYSTIFYING MAZE

Help this policeman capture Count Olaf,
who is fleeing in his car.

# CONVOLUTED CRAFT
## Make a sign to protest the mistreatment of orphans by villains.

*Step 1.* Use a photocopying machine to blow up the image on the opposite page by 556%.

*Step 2.* Using a black magic marker, write one of the following slogans on the blown-up image. You may also choose to use an appropriate message of your own devising if you think these are not very good.

> "2 Young 2 B Sad"
>
> "If you think Count Olaf is a breakfast cereal, a pleasant guardian, or a European diplomat, I'm sorry to tell you that I have some very disappointing news."
>
> "Where are the unicorns?"
>
> "Kidnapping, Theft, Arson, Bad Breath, Fraud, Murder, Poor Hygiene, Overacting . . . Guilty on Every Count!"
>
> "Baudelaire?? Baud-unfair!!"
>
> "GET OLAF (a better nose hair trimmer)"
>
> "The World Is Quiet Here"

*Step 3.* Ask your parent or guardian if you have permission to use a hacksaw.

*Step 4.* Saw off the leg of a dining room table.

*Step 5.* Affix your sign to the severed table leg using duct tape.

*Step 6.* At suppertime, walk around the table with your protest sign. Do not be alarmed if food is on the floor; food commonly surrounds tables that have had a leg removed. Do not sit down, and do not answer questions unless they are from the press.

# LABORIOUS LANGUAGE GAME

Once you've found and circled all of these words, a vital message will remain. You may search diagonally and backwards.

| | |
|---|---|
| ACTOR | LEECH |
| BANKER | PROCHRONISM |
| HERPETOLOGIST | REALTOR |
| INVENTION | INJUSTICE |
| ATLAS | VIPER |
| FORTUNE | LONGANIMITY |
| MAJUSCULE | ORPHAN |
| BAD | MARRIAGE |
| HEBDOMADAL | PUTTANESCA |
| BALD | SAILBOAT |
| HURRICANE | QUINQUENNIAL |

```
M S I N O R H C O R P L A L
E N U T R O F T I U A L T O
W A Y O R S A N T I H S B N
C A T P R O V T N E I E A G
R C H Y B E A N B G R N N A
A A A L N N E D O O S A K N
N N I T E U O L T E A C E I
X A I S Q M O L T R L I R M
S O C N A T A A D I T R E I
N A I D E E B A L D A R P T
S U A P R G H C E E L U I Y
Q L R E G A I R R A M H V B
U E I N J U S T I C E I S A
H E E L U C S U J A M ! ! D
```

_ _ _ _ _ _   _ _ _ _ _   _ _

_ _ _ _ _   _ _ _ _ _ _ _ !!

# PERPLEXING PICTURE

Find the snakes in this picture.

# MUDDLING MATH TASK

Using the information below, figure out how Olaf and his acting troupe would divide up the Baudelaire fortune if they ever got their greedy hands on it.

• The total fortune is 130 shoeboxes filled with golf ball–sized diamonds. (Both the size and nature of the fortune have been changed to protect it from the guilty.)

• The Hook-Handed Man and The Person of Indeterminate Gender get the same number of shoeboxes.

• The Bald-Headed Man gets 10 more boxes than the Hook-Handed Man.

• Count Olaf gets twice as many shoeboxes as the Bald-Headed Man.

# ENIGMATIC ENIGMA

In the field is a cow that you suspect is not a cow at all, but a spy in disguise. Nearby are two farmers, one who always lies and one who always tells the truth. What single question could you ask either one of them to find out if that cow is really a cow?

# TERMINAL TRIVIA

List all of the countries in Africa in alphabetical order. Do not get any wrong.

_____  _____  _____
_____  _____  _____
_____  _____  _____
_____  _____  _____
_____  _____  _____
_____  _____  _____
_____  _____  _____
_____  _____  _____
_____  _____  _____
_____  _____  _____
_____  _____  _____
_____  _____  _____
_____  _____  _____
_____  _____  _____
_____  _____  _____
_____  _____

# PERPLEXING PICTURE

Combine these lines to recreate a drawing of me that appeared in THE DAILY PUNCTILIO.

# ENIGMATIC ENIGMA

Use the clues to unscramble each of these words and discover a secret code that is absolutely vital for you to know.

To spy: bovrees __ _(_)_ __ __ __ __

Read _____ the lines: newbete _(_)_ __ __ __ __ __

Metallic noisemakers: lebls (_)_ __ __ __ __

Every: ahec _(_)_ __

Not the twelfth: elneveht _(_)_ __ __ __ __ __ __

What "this" is: rdow __ __ _(_)_

# CONVOLUTED CRAFT

Follow these instructions to make an almost
worthless item that only a member of a
secret organization would ever want.

*Step 1.* Pour yourself a glass of water.

*Step 2.* Spill it on the floor.

*Step 3.* Clean up the spill using paper towel.

*Step 4.* Repeat Steps 1–3 until you have nothing but a paper
towel roll and an empty glass.

*Step 5.* Hide the glass under your bed.

*Step 6.* Use a piece of coal to decorate the outside of the
paper towel roll.

*Step 7.* Use tweezers, a stick, and a piece of coal to decorate
the inside of the paper towel roll.

*Step 8.* Ask your local glasscutter for a small piece of
cellophane, also called plastic wrap,
also called "peasant's glass."

*Step 9.* Stretch the small piece of cellophane
over one end of the paper towel roll.

*Step 10.* Using glue, a stapler, a rubber band, spit, psychic ability, chewing gum, or the self-adhesive properties of plastic wrap, affix the cellophane to the paper towel roll.

*Step 11.* Hold the open end of the paper towel roll up to your eye and attempt to look through it. If you can see through the other end, you are not blind.

*Step 12.* Remove the paper towel roll from your eye and look in a mirror. If your eye is surrounded by a black ring, begin again.

*Step 13.* Observe the world carefully through your spyglass. Beware those in disguise.

# ENIGMATIC ENIGMA

Use the compass and directions to discover where Count Olaf is hiding so you can avoid the area entirely.

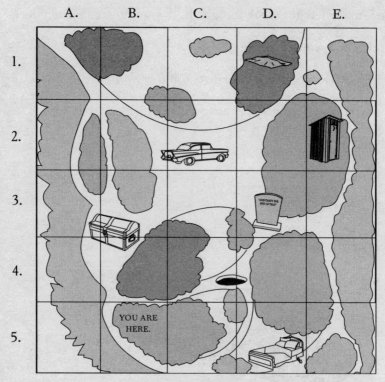

|    | A. | B. | C. | D. | E. |
|----|----|----|----|----|----|
| 1. | | | | | |
| 2. | | | | | |
| 3. | | | | | |
| 4. | | | | | |
| 5. | | | | | |

YOU ARE HERE.

Go N one block
Go NW one block
Go E one block
Go SE two blocks
Go N one block
Go NE one block
Go W one block
Go N one block
Go E one block

# PERPLEXING PICTURE

Look at this page for exactly thirty seconds, and then turn to the picture on the following page and circle the nine things that have changed. If you turn back to this page, you will be cheating, which is only appropriate in certain circumstances.

# PERPLEXING PICTURE

Look at this page for exactly one minute, and
then turn to the picture on the preceding page and
circle the nine things that have changed. If you
turn back to this page, you will be cheating, which
is only appropriate in certain circumstances.

# LABORIOUS LANGUAGE GAME

Match each of these common expressions
with their meanings.

A. Let the cat out of the bag

B. Close but no cigar

C. Foam at the mouth

D. Piece of cake

E. Red herring

1. Almost, but at least you won't smell like an ashtray

2. Easy as pie

3. Reveal a secret that may put you and every member of your secret organization in danger

4. To be very angry, especially about having to brush your teeth

5. Something intended to distract spies from the secret messages that are actually important

# MUDDLING MATH TASK

Assume Elf A and Elf B, who live at opposite ends of the enchanted forest, have nothing better to do, or that they have heard all of the other elves are gathering for a giggle convention, or that all of the woodland animals they know have grown sick of them. As a result, they sing a happy song.

Then, Elf A skips toward Elf B at 2 miles per hour, while Elf B skips toward Elf A at 3 miles per hour. The forest is 173 miles wide. Which elf will be closer to the edge of the forest when they meet?

# PERPLEXING PICTURE

As you may know, Count Olaf has a tattoo of an eye on his ankle. See if you can find the matching eyes in this picture.

# TERMINAL TRIVIA

What is the capital of Canada?

What is the capital of Latvia?

What is the capital of San Marino?

What are the capitals of the Marshall Islands?

# ENIGMATIC ENIGMA

Put each of the scrambled letters in the
right place to find what is unquestionably
THE MOST IMPORTANT SECRET
MESSAGE IN THIS ENTIRE BOOK.
All of the letters fit in spaces under their own
columns.

| H T | A E H | R I | R S R | I E | I N D | S G |
|-----|-------|-----|-------|-----|-------|-----|
|     |       |     |       | ■   |       |     |
| ■   |       | ■   |       |     |       | ■   |
|     |       |     |       |     |       |     |

# LABORIOUS LANGUAGE GAME

Fill in the blanks to complete all of these words,
which begin how Beatrice ended up.

1. Due date: dead __ __ __ __

2. Pretending to be serious: dead __ __ __

3. When agreement cannot be reached: dead __ __ __ __

4. Fatal: dead __ __

# TERMINAL TRIVIA

### Contretemps is:

a. what a stopwatch does

b. French

c. the opposite of protemps

d. a city in Switzerland

e. a word that means an unfortunate occurrence

f. the plural form of contretemps

g. a, c, and d

h. b, c, e, and f

i. b, d, and e

j. b, e, and f

k. all of the above

# CONVOLUTED CRAFT

When she is inventing something, Violet
Baudelaire ties her hair up to keep it out of the
way. Using these knots, tie your hair up to
avoid distraction while inventing.

The Fool's Knot

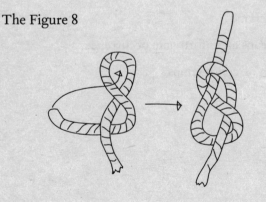

The Figure 8

# The Sheepshank

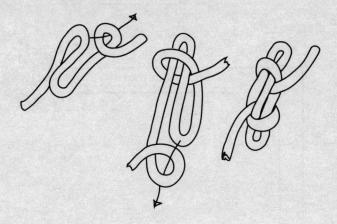

# The Monkey Fist

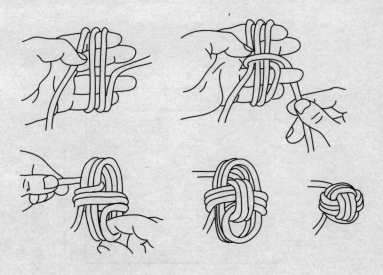

# MYSTIFYING MAZE

Help the Littlest Elf find the pretty unicorn.

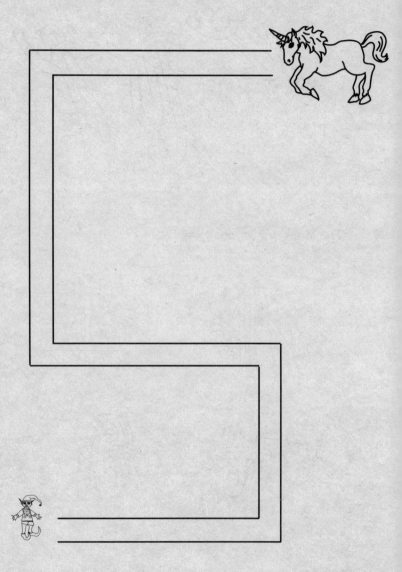

# ENIGMATIC ENIGMA

You find yourself alone in a villain's secret lair. On a table you see six file folders smudged with ketchup and fingerprints. You hear someone approaching, and have time to grab only three folders before you escape. Which ones should you take?

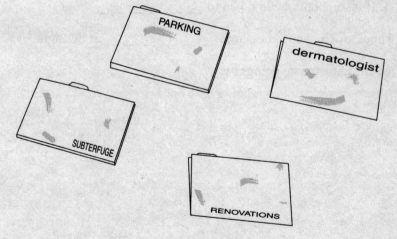

# LABORIOUS LANGUAGE GAME

For each sentence, find the one word
that makes sense in <u>both</u> blanks.

If you are forced to attend the movie *Lemony Snicket's A Series of Unfortunate Events*:

1. No matter what, __ __ __ __ __ __ your eyes from the film showing on the __ __ __ __ __ __.

2. __ __ __ __ for the door, or cut a blindfold from an enormous __ __ __ __ of black blindfold cloth.

3. If all else fails, bend down to __ __ __ __ __ __ your shoes, or else your knees may __ __ __ __ __ __ at the sight of the unfortunate goings on.

# PERPLEXING PICTURE

Circle the things that are wrong in this picture.

# TERMINAL TRIVIA

What ball-shaped knot makes it easy to throw a
rope across the gap between two buildings?
This can be very useful if you are trying to
heave a heavy object like a baby from
one rooftop to another.

# MUDDLING MATH TASK

The Littlest Elf has been giggling at nothing for
the entire 32 years he has been alive. The pretty
unicorn is 120 years old. How old will the pretty
unicorn be when she is exactly twice as old as
the Littlest Elf?

# PERPLEXING PICTURE

Decipher these combinations of pictures and
letters to find out places where bad news
is likely to appear.

1.

2.

3.

# ENIGMATIC ENIGMA

Color in every letter below that is not a V, an F, or a D to discover the secret message.

```
V  F  R  D  E  D  V  P
F  D  L  D  D  A  V  V
C  D  F  E  F  V  T  V
F  H  D  V  E  F  D  B
F  D  A  F  T  T  D  E
V  F  D  R  V  I  F  D
E  S  I  D  N  F  Y  D
V  O  F  D  F  V  D  U
F  R  D  V  S  V  D  M
O  F  V  D  K  F  V  E
A  D  F  V  L  A  D
V  F  V  D  V  R  F
D  V  F  M  V  D
```

_ _ _ _ _ _ _   _ _ _   _ _ _ _ _ _ _ _ _

_ _   _ _ _ _   _ _ _ _ _   _ _ _ _ _

# MUDDLING MATH TASK

Count Olaf is in the process of doing something terrible you'd prefer not to know about when he is interrupted by the authorities and escapes. He runs 50 feet to a secret tunnel, crawls 430 yards underground, jumps into a waiting getaway car, drives 72 miles, boards a train and travels 40 furlongs, and jauntily walks 3 rods to a convenience store, where he drinks an orange pop. How far away is he from the scene of the crime?

| |
|---|
| 3 feet = 1 yard |
| 5.5 yards = 1 rod |
| 40 rods = 1 furlong |
| 8 furlongs = 1 mile |

a) 407,949.5 feet

b) 135,983.16 yards

c) 24,724.21 rods

d) 618.11 furlongs

e) 77.26 miles

# CONVOLUTED CRAFT

Build a sailboat, which is of no use whatsoever
because it is made of paper
and is too small for you to sit in.

*Step 1.* Take one page from *The Daily Punctilio*, which was once a well-respected newspaper but has since proven unreliable.

*Step 2.* Fold in half along the dotted lines.

*Step 3.* Fold inward along the dotted lines.

*Step 4.* There is a strip along the bottom. Fold its top flap up along the dotted line.

*Step 5.* Fold the corners back along the dotted lines.

*Step 6.* Turn the whole thing over, and fold up along the dotted line.

*Step 7.* Take a break. You have been working very hard. Your paper should look like this.

*Step 8.* Stick your thumbs inside and pull.

*Step 9.* If you haven't given up yet, your paper should look like this. Fold the top flap of the bottom half up along the dotted line.

*Step 10.* You must be exhausted. Your paper should look like this. Now turn the whole thing over.

*Step 11.* Repeat Step 9.

*Step 12.* Repeat Step 8.

*Step 13.* Now would be a good time to quit. Pull the corners as shown.

*Step 14.* You have succeeded. Put on your head and wear only in emergencies, or at designated official meetings.

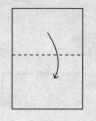

**2.**

**3.**

**4.**

**5.**

**6.**

**7.**

**8.**

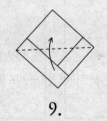

**9.**

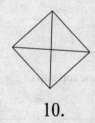

**10.**

**13.**

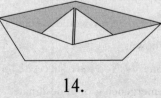

**14.**

# PERPLEXING PICTURE

Put the following events in the order they occurred.

A.

B.

C.

D.

E.

# LABORIOUS LANGUAGE GAME

Unscramble these words to find things that you
probably want to avoid for the rest of your life.

1. suirhracen _ _ _ _ _ _ _ _ _ _

2. andokhomedanh

_ _ _ _ -_ _ _ _ _ _    _ _ _

3. cyseellarmosheech

_ _ _ _ _ _ _ _ _ _    _ _ _ _ _ _ _

4. buccumserupo _ _ _ _ _ _ _ _    _ _ _ _

5. lemonysnicketsaseriesofunfortunatesvente

_ _ _ _ _ _    _ _ _ _ _ _ _ '_ _

_ _ _ _ _ _    _ _    _ _ _ _ _ _ _ _ _ _ _

_ _ _ _ _ _

# TERMINAL TRIVIA

Which word in this specially constructed sentence is commonly pronounced incorrectly by most people, including citizens, educators, children, and postal clerks?

# MUDDLING MATH TASK

There are eight bankers.
Three have a cough, four have top hats, and two have both.
How many bankers are healthy and hatless?

# PERPLEXING PICTURE

Study this picture for exactly one minute. Then turn the page and take a quiz about it.

## 1. Who is the artist who drew this picture?

a. Brett Helquist

b. Lucille Ball

c. Otto Handler

d. Meredith Heuer

e. Biff Nussbaum

## 2. What color are the maitre d's socks?

a. Black

b. White

c. Blue

d. Yellow

e. Purple

## 3. What time of day is it in this picture?

a. Mid-morning

b. Mid-late morning

c. Early afternoon

d. Thick of night

e. Suppertime

## 4. Why does the young woman look ill?

a. Poor lighting

b. The Surprising Chicken Salad

c. Pneumonia

d. Tongue sticking out

## 5. How many clowns are there in this picture?

a. 0

b. 1

c. 2

d. 3

e. 44

# ENIGMATIC ENIGMA

To decipher this secret code, start at the O on the
outer edge and travel into the center of the eye,
collecting all of the letters in the shaded areas.
Upon reaching the center, you should run for your
life, collecting all of the letters in the white areas
on your way out.

Start

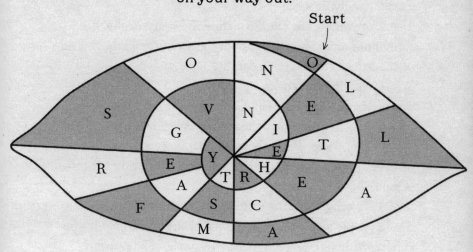

\_\_\_\_ \_\_\_\_ _____

\_\_\_ _____

# CONVOLUTED CRAFT

Aunt Josephine gave Violet Baudelaire a doll named Pretty Penny. Dress Pretty Penny up in a pretty outfit, if you like that sort of thing.

*Step 1.* Ask your parent or guardian if you have permission to use the family jig saw.

*Step 2.* If you do, cut out the picture of Pretty Penny. Be careful not to accidentally cut out the activities on the flip side of the page.

*Step 3.* Cut out the outfits.

*Step 4.* Using a stapler, staple an outfit to Pretty Penny.

*Step 5.* Play a nice game of make-believe. For instance, you might make Pretty Penny bake an imaginary cake using mud or have her go to the big dance with another boring cut-out person.

*Step 6.* To remove Penny's outfit, use a staple remover.

*Step 7.* Staple a new outfit to Pretty Penny. Note that if you choose the bikini, you will need two staples, and possibly three.

*Step 8.* Repeat steps 4–7 until you become extremely bored. You may even begin to read sentences over and over because you are having difficulty paying attention.

*Step 9.* Repeat steps 4–7 until you become extremely bored. You may even begin to read sentences over and over because you are having difficulty paying attention.

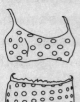

# LABORIOUS LANGUAGE GAME

A palindrome is a word or sentence that reads the same both forwards and backwards, like "racecar." Figure out the missing letters in each of the following palindromes.

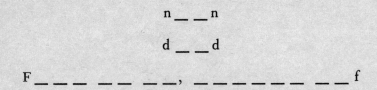

n_ _ _ n

d _ _ d

F_ _ _ _ _ _ _, _ _ _ _ _ _ _ _ f

# ENIGMATIC ENIGMA

Match the book Klaus Baudelaire is reading with the information he is likely to find in it.

1. *The Wonderful World of Math*

2. *Algebra II*

3. *Complex Division Brings Us Together*

4. *Fractions in Action!*

5. *When Fun Multiplies*

a. 3, 5, 7, and 11 are all prime numbers.

b. Ants are the enemies of bees.

c. Prairie dogs aren't actually dogs.

d. Cats clean themselves with their tongues.

e. Mice are filthy animals.

# TERMINAL TRIVIA

What are the major cuts of veal?
Be sure to include the foreshank.

_____        _____

_____        _____

_____        _____

_____        _____

_____        _____

_____

# PERPLEXING PICTURE

Identify seven differences between the people in these two pictures.

A.

B.

# LABORIOUS LANGUAGE GAME

Fill in the names of age-appropriate toys for
Sunny Baudelaire to play with.

# ENIGMATIC ENIGMA

Find the coded message in this excerpt from the screenplay for the film SURGEONS IN THE THEATER by Dr. Gustav Sebald. You may choose to use the Sebald Code, unless you are a villain, in which case you should use the Helquist Code.

(A bell rings)

### DR. NIETZCHE

Be still, while I cut into your— Wait! What was that!? Quiet, you! Don't you know all bells should be turned off when you are attending the theater!? How rude!!

### YOUNG ROLF

What, ho? Are you talking to me? That wasn't my bell, fool!

### AUDIENCE MEMBER #17

Shhhh! You are ruining it for everybody!

### YOUNG ROLF

Me?! He's the one who is attempting to operate on someone during the show!

### DR. NIETZCHE

How dare you! To intensive care I'll send you!! What kind of man would eavesdrop in a theater!

(A bell rings)

### DR. BROWN

Shhhh! All of you!!! I'm trying to remove a spleen over here!

# MYSTIFYING MAZE

Help me find peace.

Start ↘

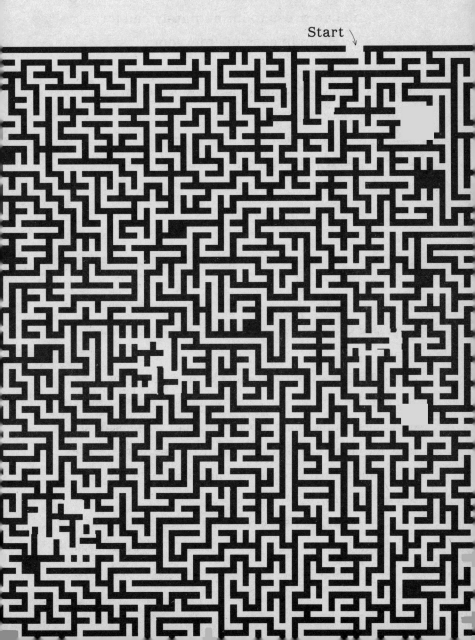

# CONVOLUTED CRAFT

Construct a panic button, which is something
you can press to immediately call for
help in case of emergency.

*Step 1.* You will need a small paper cup, of the sort used in
dentists' offices for gargling liquids. Go find one.

*Step 2.* Good. Now paint your small paper cup bright red, like
a fire engine. If your paper cup is already bright red, please
return it to its rightful owner and make your own, unless they
told you it was okay for you to take their panic button.

*Step 3.* Decide on the location of your panic button. Next to
your pillow is a common choice, because many people believe
that surprising things are most likely to happen in the middle
of the night, when they are sleeping. In truth, far more
surprising things happen during the day, when everybody is
awake.

*Step 4.* Decide where you would like the panic button to be
connected in case of emergency. Many people choose the fire
department or the police department, but I can think of at
least one instance in which they were too late. Some people
choose their parents' room, assuming their parents are not
terrible villains.

*Step 5.* Measure the distance between the chosen location of
your panic button and the place to which it will be connected
in case of emergency. If the place you are connecting to is

relatively far away, as the nearest Coast Guard office can be, it may be helpful to wear good walking shoes for this step.

*Step 6.* Cut a piece of string of the length arrived at in Step 5.

*Step 7.* Tape one end of the string to the bottom of your paper cup.

*Step 8.* Tie the other end of the string to a metal fork or, if necessary, a spoon.

*Step 9.* Place the silverware inside a small metal saucepan in the location you would like to notify in case of emergency. For instance, you might put the saucepan with the "emergency fork" in it under your sister's bed.

*Step 10.* Using black electrical tape, masking tape colored black with a magic marker, gray tape spray-painted black, or tar, affix the panic button to your chosen place. Make sure you don't tape over the string, and that the string is taut.

*Step 11.* In case of emergency, press the panic button! Be sure to completely depress the button, crushing the cup. This will cause a sudden slackening of the string connecting your panic button to the authorities, which will cause a clanking sound. Assuming, of course, that you measured the distance correctly. And that no speeding automobiles, closing doors, foolish pets, or tripping people break the string or set off a false alarm or jam the whole device. Also, someone has to be listening.

*Step 12.* In fact, you're probably better off yelling loudly in case of emergency. Running also sometimes helps.

# ENIGMATIC ENIGMA

You are conducting secret research in Paltryville
when a gray train passes slowly nearby. You
notice that there are big letters on each freight
car. You have a sneaking suspicion that someone
is trying to tell you something, but that the
freight cars may have gotten mixed up.
Put them in the right order to
reveal an important secret saying
you should be extremely careful about saying.

# TERMINAL TRIVIA

How many letters are there in
the Chinese alphabet?

# LABORIOUS LANGUAGE GAME

There's another way to
describe the following things,
using two single-syllable words that rhyme.
The first instance has been completed for you,
because sometimes an example is helpful.

1. This activity: <u>l</u> <u>a</u> <u>m</u> <u>e</u>   <u>g</u> <u>a</u> <u>m</u> <u>e</u>

2. A sharp-handed thief: __ __ __ __   __ __ __ __ __ .

3. Preferred drink of Count Olaf, many Frenchmen, and all

sommeliers: __ __ __ __   __ __ __ __

4. A depressed male person of approximately your age:

__ __ __   __ __ __

5. A phony serpent: __ __ __ __   __ __ __ __ __

6. An attempt to weep: __ __ __   __ __ __

# PERPLEXING PICTURE
## Which of these is not like the others?

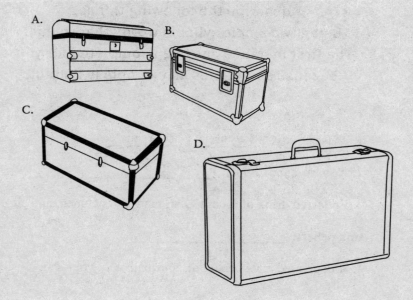

A.

B.

C.

D.

# MUDDLING MATH TASK

If Violet Baudelaire could invent a time machine
that enabled her to go back to before her parents
perished in a terrible fire and save them, how
many unfortunate events might have been
averted? Assume that the Baudelaire mansion
burnt down exactly forty-seven years ago, and
that an average of 6.4 unfortunate events have
occurred each day since then.

# CONVOLUTED CRAFT

I am sorry to say that a Scavenger Hunt is not a craft, and you will probably find it a waste of time. Having arrived at the end of this book, you are welcome to go play outside—that is, unless you want to complete your training, in which case you should locate each of the things listed below.

Your spyglass
A wedding dress
Your official hat
A sawn-off table leg
A blindfold
VFD Field Training Guide
King Tut
A box of golf ball–sized diamonds
A raw carrot
A monkey fist
A drinking glass hidden under a bed
Beef Wellington
The method for breaking the Sebald Code
Burundi
A typewriter
A giant suitcase
A scavenger hunt
A panic button

# THE ANSWERS

page 1 (Perplexing Picture):
Unfortunately, none. That is why your training is so important.


page 2 (Mystifying Maze):
Unfortunately, this maze cannot be solved at this time. If you are lucky, however, you can help the Baudelaire children find the pretty unicorn.

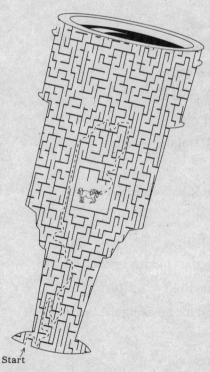

Start

page 3 (Enigmatic Enigma):
The secret message is "11." I have included the answers to each clue, in case a blindfold prevented you from simply counting the letters and blanks shown for clue #4: 1. New Zealand, 2. Wellington, 3. Crust, 4. Lithosphere

page 4 (Laborious Language Game):

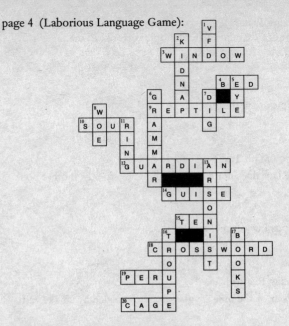

page 8 (Laborious Language Game):
1. The correct answer completes the word "gaol," which is an old British word for jail that is pronounced "jail." 2. The correct answer completes the word "laments." 3. The correct answer completes the phrase "trading looks."

page 8 (Terminal Trivia):
 85. According to census data, over 112 people with the last name "Baudelaire" currently exist. Twenty-seven of them are only children.

page 9 (Perplexing Picture):
That man is not a policeman.

page 11 (Enigmatic Enigma):
# VOLUNTEERS NEEDED PLEASE CONTINUE

page 11 (Perplexing Picture):
A. Mr. Poe, B. you, C. Count Olaf, D. Captain Hook, E. me,
F. Tutankhamen (also known as King Tut)

page 12 (Perplexing Picture):
All of these people are in disguise.

page 13 (Muddling Math Task):
Unfortunately, Klaus does not have enough money to buy another book.

page 16 (Laborious Language Game):
A lot.

page 17 (Perplexing Picture):
Unfortunately, four of the nine spyglasses are concealed by smoke and
rubble.

page 18 (Perplexing Picture):

page 19 (Mystifying Maze):
Unfortunately, this maze cannot be solved at this time. If you are lucky, however, you can help the policeman arrive at his happy home.

page 22 (Laborious Language Game):

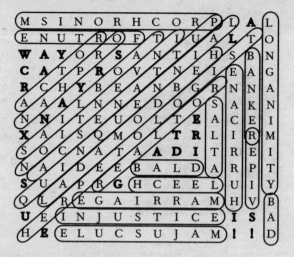

The secret message is
# ALWAYS CARRY AN EXTRA DISGUISE!!

page 24 (Perplexing Picture):

page 25 (Muddling Math Task):
Although he may only be entitled to 60 shoeboxes, Count Olaf would take the entire fortune regardless of any prior agreement.


page 26 (Enigmatic Enigma):
Ask, "What would the other farmer say if I asked him if that's really a cow?" If you ask the liar, he will lie and reply, "He'll say it's a cow"—which would mean the truthful farmer would tell you that it's *not* a cow, which is the truth. If you ask the truthful farmer, he'll say of his lying neighbor, "He'll say it's a cow."

Either way, they'll reply the same way, and you'll know that the opposite of whatever they say is true. That cow is actually a spy in disguise. The question of whether those farmers are really farmers, however, remains.


page 26 (Terminal Trivia):
Algeria, Angola, Benin, Botswana, Burkina Faso, Burundi, Cameroon, Cape Verde, Central African Republic, Chad, Comoros, Congo (Brazzaville), Congo (DRC, Zaire), Côte d'Ivoire, Djibouti, Egypt, Equatorial Guinea, Eritrea, Ethiopia, Gabon, Gambia, Ghana, Guinea, Guinea-Bissau, Kenya, Lesotho, Liberia, Libya, Madagascar, Malawi, Mali, Mauritania, Mauritius, Morocco, Mozambique, Namibia, Niger, Nigeria, Reunion, Rwanda, Sao Tome and Principe, Senegal, Seychelles, Sierra Leone, Somalia, South Africa, Sudan, Swaziland, Tanzania, Togo, Tunisia, Uganda, Western Sahara, Zambia, Zimbabwe


page 27 (Perplexing Picture):

page 27 (Enigmatic Enigma):

# OBSERVE BETWEEN BELLS EACH
# ELEVENTH WORD.

The secret code is SEBALD.

page 30 (Enigmatic Enigma):
The correct answer is block E2. Count Olaf was previously hiding in block D1, but an associate tipped him off regarding your search.

pages 31–32 (Perplexing Picture):

## PERPLEXING PICTURE:
Look at this page for exactly one minute, and then turn to the picture on the preceding page and circle the nine things that have changed. If you turn back to this page, you will be cheating, which is only appropriate in certain circumstances.

page 33 (Laborious Language Game):
A. 3, B. 1, C. 4, D. 2, E. 5


page 34 (Muddling Math Task):
This is a tiresome question, only partly because it is about singing elves.
The elves will clearly be the same distance from the edge of the forest
when they meet, because the word "meet" here means "arrive at the same
place."


page 35 (Perplexing Picture):

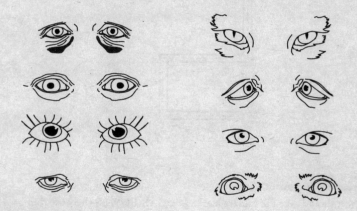


page 36 (Terminal Trivia):
Ottawa, Riga, San Marino, M and I


page 36 (Enigmatic Enigma):
# THIS IS A RED HERRING

page 37 (Laborious Language Game):
1. deadline, 2. deadpan, 3. deadlock, 4. deadly


Page 37 (Terminal Trivia):
j


page 40 (Mystifying Maze):
Hooray!

page 41 (Enigmatic Enigma):
You should take the folders marked SUGAR BOWLS (because they
frequently contain important information), FULMINATIONS (because
it is a word which means explosions), and SUBTERFUGE (because it
indicates a dastardly scheme). That is, unless you are interested in where a
villain's car may be parked, who is responsible for their skin care, or what
sort of tile they are planning to install in their washroom.


page 42 (Laborious Language Game):
1. screen, 2. bolt, 3. buckle

page 43 (Perplexing Picture):
• The sailor is not wearing a life jacket.
• There is a hole in the
  side of the boat.
• There is a sandwich
  on deck, which is sure to
  attract Lachrymose Leeches.
• The sailor is wearing
  a blindfold.
• The sail is on fire.
• The Dirigible Mooring Station
  has been covered in
  broadcasting equipment.
• Shark!
• Sailing in a hurricane
  is a terrible idea,
  unless you are trying to find your
  missing guardian before it's too late.

page 44 (Terminal Trivia):
The monkey fist.

page 44 (Muddling Math Task):
To figure out when one person or mythical creature will be twice as old
as another, simply double the age difference between them. Since the
unicorn is 88 years older than the Littlest Elf, she will be twice as old as
the Elf when she is 176 years old and the Elf is 88. There is no need to
worry, however, since neither is likely to live that long.

page 45 (Perplexing Picture):
1. Briny Beach, 2. *Daily Punctilio*, 3. movie theater

page 46 (Enigmatic Enigma):

# REPLACE THE BATTERIES IN YOUR SMOKE ALARM

page 47 (Muddling Math Task):

a, b, c, d, and e are all correct.

page 50 (Perplexing Picture):

The correct order is D, E, A, C, B. The Littlest Elf rode the pretty unicorn to Pleasant Pond and decided to splash about. The unicorn returned to the village and picked up the Littlest Elf's cousin, commonly known as "He's also very little," and brought him back to share in the fun. The unicorn then sunbathed. One thousand years later, a tree grew on that very spot!

page 51 (Laborious Language Game):

1. hurricanes, 2. Hook-Handed Man, 3. Lachrymose Leeches, 4. cucumber soup, 5. *Lemony Snicket's A Series of Unfortunate Events*

page 52 (Terminal Trivia):

"incorrectly"

page 52 (Muddling Math Task):

Three. One way to get the right answer would be to guess. Another is to draw a diagram like the one on the next page. As you can see, five bankers have a cough, a top hat, or both—which leaves three left over who have neither. Unfortunately, however, a hatless banker is likely to catch a bad cough soon enough.

BANKERS WITH A COUGH    BANKERS WITH A HAT

pages 53–54 (Perplexing Picture):
1. e, 2. d, 3. c, 4. d, 5. c

page 55 (Enigmatic Enigma):

## OLAF SEES EVERYTHING ACT NORMAL

page 58 (Laborious Language Game):
noon; deed; Flee to me, remote elf

page 58 (Enigmatic Enigma):
1. a, 2. a, 3. a, 4. a, 5. a

page 59 (Terminal Trivia):
Foreshank, arm, neck, blade, rib (rack), loin, sirloin, rump, round,
hindshank, tip, flank, breast

page 60 (Perplexing Picture):

B is an excellent speller.

A is wearing a brown skirt, while B is wearing green slacks.

A's foot hurts.

B has a birthmark on his elbow.

A's coat has three buttons, while B's coat has four.

A is taller.

B is wearing an eye patch.


page 61 (Laborious Language Game):

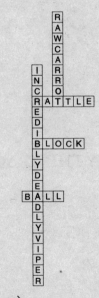

page 62 (Enigmatic Enigma):

(A bell rings)


## DR. NIETZCHE

Be still, while I cut into your— Wait! What was that!? Quiet, you! Don't you know all bells should be turned off when you are attending the theater!? How rude!!

### YOUNG ROLF

What, ho? Are <u>you</u> talking to me? That wasn't my bell, fool!

### AUDIENCE MEMBER #17

Shhhh! You <u>are</u> ruining it for everybody!

### YOUNG ROLF

Me?! He's the one who is <u>attempting</u> to operate on someone during the show!

### DR. NIETZCHE

How dare you! <u>To</u> intensive care I'll send you!! What kind of man would <u>eavesdrop</u> in a theater!

(A bell rings)

### DR. BROWN

Shhhh! All of you!!! I'm trying to remove a spleen over here!

The coded message is BE QUIET WHEN YOU ARE ATTEMPTING TO EAVESDROP

page 63 (Mystifying Maze):
It is kind of you to try.

page 66 (Enigmatic Enigma):
THE WORLD IS QUIET HERE

page 66 (Terminal Trivia): There are 18 letters in the phrase "the Chinese alphabet."

page 67 (Laborious Language Game):
1. hook crook, 2. fine wine, 3. sad lad, 4. fake snake, 5. cry try

page 68 (Perplexing Picture):
While all of the other pieces of luggage pictured are empty, someone is locked inside trunk C. Please send help right away.


page 68 (Muddling Math Task):
Assuming that each year has 365 days, approximately 109,792 unfortunate events might never have happened, and this book is only one of them.


page 69 (Convoluted Craft):
All of these items may be located by rifling through different neighbors' homes and traveling to Africa, but probably not. If you were successful, it was almost certainly by completing each of the activities within this book. If that is the case, solemn congratulations are in order. Please immediately see the typographical error at the end of this book for further instructions.


A spyglass—pages 2, 17, 28–9
A wedding dress—pages 12
The official hat—pages 32, 48–49
A sawn-off table leg—pages 20–21
A blindfold—pages 6–7, 12, 43
VFD Field Training Guide—pages 1–69
King Tut—page 11
A box of golf ball–sized diamonds—page 25
A panic button—pages 64–65
A raw carrot—page 61
A monkey fist—pages 39, 44
A drinking glass hidden under a bed—page 28
Beef Wellington—page 3
The method for breaking the Sebald Code—pages 4–5, 27, 62
Burundi—page 26
A typewriter—pages 31–32
A giant suitcase—page 68
A scavenger hunt—page 69

# NOTES

# NOTES

# NOTES

# NOTES

If you are a spying villain or a villainous spy, we're sorry to tell you that this entire page is a typographical error, a phrase which here means "a silly mistake that is of no importance whatsoever, so you should quickly turn this book right side up and continue snooping around the Answers as Far as I Know." If you are a volunteer, however, we would like to extend a sigh of relief. You have successfully completed your elementary training. In most dangerous, dire, deceptive, or very boring situations, the skills now at your disposal will prove infinitely valuable, both to you and to those we must do everything we can to help. These skills include Arithmetic (1,667.79), Concealment (see underneath your bed), Cooking (knowing one's way around the kitchen drastically reduces the chance of burning), Crisis Management, Detail Recognition and Comprehension (clue = detail in disguise), Disguise Preparation and Detection (n.b. adversaries may be using same disguises as allies), Eye Obstruction (blindfold, eye patch), Financial Analysis ($1,667.79), Following Instructions (keep reading), Geography, Knot-tying (advanced), Letter Unscrambling (see Al Funcoot), Logical Reasoning, Map Reading and Mistrust, Maze Navigation, Measurement (including furlongs), Origami (Japanese paper-folding art which has many applications, including the construction of emergency vehicles and swans), Parts of Speech, Patience, Political Activism (especially the use of nonviolent protest as a productive force for social change), Quick Thinking, Reading (see A Series of Unfortunate Events by Lemony Snicket), Sebald Code Transmission and Deduction (to prevent miscommunication, avoid accidental and indiscriminate use of doorbells, jingle bells, barbells, bellbottoms, etc.), Slow Thinking, Spontaneous Secret Message Analysis (SSMA), Spyglass Construction (quick method), and Suspicion. The next phase of your education will include sugar bowl excavation. Look for the black jeep. Keep this field training guide on your person at all times, including when you are in the bath or shower. All cannot be lost when there is still so much being found. The world is quiet here. Welcome.